The Adventures of Francis Bear & Yellow Duck

The Great Asteroid Rescue

Craig Horan
&
Catherine Rothwell

MAPLE
PUBLISHERS

The Adventures of Francis Bear & Little Yellow Duck – The Great Asteroid Rescue

Author: Craig Horan & Catherine Rothwell

First Published in 2023

ISBN: 978-1-915492-90-6 (Paperback)

Book cover design, Illustrations and Book layout by:
White Magic Studios
www.whitemagicstudios.co.uk

Published by:
Maple Publishers
Fairbourne Drive, Atterbury,
Milton Keynes,
MK10 9RG, UK
www.maplepublishers.com

A CIP catalogue record for this title is available from the British Library.

It was a sunny day down by the canal. Francis Bear and Little Yellow Duck were sitting on their favourite bench, watching the barges go by, the ducks were playing in the water.

Alfie was curled up asleep under the bench.

"Wouldn't it be fantastic to fly high into the sky and explore the stars and planets?" Francis Bear pondered as he gazed up into the blue sky.

"Quack! Quack!" agreed Little Yellow Duck.

"Let's go to the Space Centre!" exclaimed Francis Bear, as he jumped off the bench with excitement.

Alfie barked and Little Yellow Duck quacked.

The three friends headed off along the tow path towards the bus stop at the end of the path, Alfie leading the way.

After a short bus ride, they were soon outside the Space Centre.

The revolving doors at the entrance were breath-taking, each door had a different spaceship painted on it.

Francis Bear spun the door until their favourite spaceship, the Jupiter II, appeared. Then the three friends jumped in.

Once inside the Space Centre they were
all amazed at the fabulous display of
spaceships, space suits, planets and stars!

"How awesome is this!" said Francis Bear,
as he ran over to a space suit and wished he
had one of his own.

Ping! Pong! "The next Starry Sky Show in our planetarium will begin in five minutes."

Francis Bear recognised the voice immediately, it was Professor Pallas, THE space expert.

Alfie ran off down the corridor. He knew where he was going.

As the show started, the lights dimmed, the room went dark and the stars were sparkling overhead. "It is magical" said Francis Bear.

Professor Pallas made the journey into space sound very exciting. Alfie however, had found a warm spot and was soon curled up fast asleep.

After the show Francis Bear and Little Yellow Duck pretended to be astronauts, talking to mission control and walking in slow motion like real astronauts on the moon.

The spaceship hanger was the next stop.

Slowly, slowly, Francis Bear and Little Yellow Duck walked into the enormous hanger with the spaceships on display.

"Can you imagine the thrilling adventures these spaceships have had?" said Francis Bear.

Their favourite spaceship Jupiter II was parked at the end of the row, it had always been flown by the famous astronaut, Major Athena Banks.

They ran to the Jupiter II, climbed the ladder into the cockpit. Put their space helmets on and pretended they were flying into space.

Suddenly! The three friends heard on their helmet radios a voice saying "Mayday! Mayday!" They stopped their game and listened carefully.

"Mayday! Mayday! This is Bluebird IV. We are on an asteroid and our rocket engines have failed."

"We have to help." said Francis Bear to his friends. Little Yellow Duck quacked; Alfie barked in agreement.

Francis Bear adjusted his headset radio and said, "Blue Bird IV, this is Francis Bear and crew, we are on our way to rescue you."

Francis Bear turned to Little Yellow Duck and Alfie and said,

"Buckle up, get ready for take-off, we're now on a rescue mission!"

"Ground Control, this is Jupiter II, we are ready for take-off." announced Francis Bear

"You are clear for take-off." said a voice from Ground Control. As the countdown started the roof of the hanger opened, revealing the blue sky.

"This is it" exclaimed Francis Bear, "we are going into space!"

Francis Bear was trying to control his excitement.

And the final countdown began:
10......9......8......7......6......5......4......3......2......1......

Francis Bear pulled back the red handle.

There was a huge roar from the spaceship's engines and Whoosh! Francis Bear skilfully guided the spaceship through the open roof, flying through the clouds and into the immense darkness of space.

"It's so quiet." Whispered Francis Bear. Little Yellow Duck flapped her wings and Alfie wagged his tail at the wonder of everything before them.

Radio contact had been lost with Blue Bird IV but luckily ground control had sent the directions for the asteroid to Francis Bear.

Ahead through the trail of stars was the glow of the asteroid. Standing next to a red and gold spaceship was a figure waving frantically.

Dressed in his space suit Francis Bear went into the air locked door chamber. Little Yellow Duck sealed the doors behind him.

Francis Bear carefully climbed out onto the asteroid.

As he got nearer, Francis Bear saw that the astronaut was the world-famous, Major Athena Banks.

Francis Bear was so excited to see Major Banks but there was no time to chat. On the way, Francis Bear had already come up with a rescue plan. He quickly explained it to Major Banks.

Francis Bear carefully attached towing lines from Jupiter II to Blue Bird IV. He gently raised the Jupiter II up off the asteroid, pulling the Blue Bird IV safely behind.

Towing the Blue Bird IV was hard work. Little Yellow Duck and Alfie sat quietly behind Francis Bear.

"Don't worry Little Yellow Duck," reassured Francis Bear, "we will soon be back home."

"Look!" exclaimed Francis Bear, as the Space Centre landing pads started to come into view.

The landing parachutes of both spaceships launched at the same time, which caused the ships to shake and judder and slow down very quickly.

Francis Bear and Major Banks skilfully landed their spaceships onto the landing pads.

The news had travelled quickly about the asteroid rescue and a large crowd, including his Majesty the King, had gathered to welcome the heroes back to earth.

Francis Bear, Little Yellow
Duck and Major Banks stood
on top of the steps to their
spaceships and waved to the
cheering crowds. Alfie barked
and wagged his tail.

The King presented the
three heroes with a lifetime
membership to the Space
Centre and their very own
space suits.

"What a day!" yawned Francis Bear who was wearing his space suit. "I can't wait for our next adventure!"

"Quack! Quack!" said Little Yellow Duck.

"Woof! Woof!" barked Alfie.

Ingram Content Group UK Ltd.
Milton Keynes UK
UKHW021608050523
421274UK00007B/33